PZ
10.3
.F8855
W .3
Freschet
The web in the grass

2-WEEK RESERVE:
NO RENEWAL

The Web in the Grass

The Web in the Grass

By Berniece Freschet

Illustrated by Roger Duvoisin

CHARLES SCRIBNER'S SONS
NEW YORK

Text Copyright© 1972 Berniece Freschet
Illustrations Copyright© 1972 Roger Duvoisin

A-9.72 [RZ]

Printed in the United States of America
Library of Congress Catalog Card Number 72-1165
SBN 684-12956-6 (cloth, RB)

For Maria, with special love

A soft spring wind blew across the green meadow.
Close to the earth, hidden in the cool, dark grasses,
a small spider spun a shiny thread.
Her world was filled with enemies.
The small spider had no friends.

Her legs were long and slender, and on her handsome black coat were bright orange spots.

Because she was hungry, she began to make a web.

Spinning thread out behind her, the small spider fastened her silken lines to the leaves and rocks and blades of grass.

These filmy threads of gossamer were finer than even those of the silkworm.

The spider ran back and forth, back and forth.

Never stopping.

Never resting.

The long lines of shining threads crossed, and crossed again until they looked like the spokes of a wheel.

Starting at the center of the spokes, the spider began to walk around the lines in a circle.

Around and around she went.
The circles got bigger and bigger.
At the edge of the web, she turned and went back.
Now she spun a sticky thread.
The circles got smaller and smaller.
Finally she stopped.

A beautiful web of gossamer lace hung between the grasses.

It was so delicate that it looked as if it might blow away.

But it was very strong. This web would catch and hold a meal for the small spider.

She hid under a leaf close by.

She waited.

A cricket chirruped.
KRIC-KET   KRIC-KET

Something rustled through the
grasses—a green snake slid past.

Near by, a butterfly came out of her chrysalis.
Slowly, very slowly, she began to unfold her wings.
The butterfly held her beautiful yellow wings out
to the warm sun to dry.
Before long she flew away.

The small spider waited.

A wasp flew near. This was the spider's most dangerous enemy.

The wasp began to hunt under leaves and twigs and through the tangle of weeds.

She was looking for spiders.

The small spider was very still.

The wasp came close...
　　　　　　　closer....
But she did not find the spider hiding under the
leaf.
Finally the wasp droned away.

Suddenly the little spider's web began to sway.
Then the delicate strands began to jump...
                              and to shake...and to jerk....
Something was caught in the spider's trap.
She ran out to see. It was a green fly.
Quickly the spider spun her thread, wrapping it
around and around the fly. Then she carried it off,
back to her hiding place.

A jay hopped down and poked his bill into the leaves near by. He found a black beetle and winged up into the sky.

When it was safe, the spider came out to fix her web.

A fat toad sat under a leafy fern. His bulging eyes watched the busy spider at work. The hungry toad's long, sticky tongue darted out.

Quickly the spider ran up a stem and hid in the petals of a flower.

The sun went down behind the hills.

It grew dark, but still the small spider was not safe. Some animals hunted their food at night—the skunk did, and the possum.

Not far away, in the woods, lived an owl.
He could see black beetles and black spiders even
in the darkness.

That night the spider caught a mosquito in her web...

and a moth flew into her tangle of threads.

Each time the spider mended the broken strands.

Then she went back to her hiding place to wait.

All night long she waited.

The dark sky grew light.

The sun came up and shone on the silken web.

Tiny dewdrops hung there, sparkling like bright jewels caught in a fairy net.

A meadow lark sang a song to the new day.

Now the small spider began to spin a new kind of thread — she was making her egg sac.

She laid her eggs.

She spun more silk and patted it into a soft blanket around the eggs.

When she was done, the tired little spider rested under her leaf.

A titmouse poked about the grasses.

He was looking for spider eggs to eat.

But he did not see the egg sac that hung above, close against the weed stem.

In three weeks the baby spiders hatched.

They were very tiny.

Hundreds of spiderlings crowded together in the sac.

The baby spiders made a hole in the covering, and one by one, out they came, out into the bright sunshine.

The little spiders had no friends. Only a few would find a safe place to hide. This was nature's way.

The little spiders began to climb.

They climbed up blades of grass.

Up weed stems.

Up bushes and shrubs.

Up and up. To the very highest spot they could find.

Blossoms from the wild honeysuckle filled the air with a sweet smell as the baby spiders stretched out their bodies and began to spin.

Like wisps of smoke, the strands of silk drifted upward, the warm air lifting them higher and higher.

Soon hundreds of baby spiders were ballooning through the sky.

The sun shone on the silken threads
                              billowing
                    bright as new-washed silver.

The spiderlings drifted on the wind.
To places near...
                    and places far.

And wherever the baby spiders floated down...
to twig and leaf...
they spun their threads of silk.
The little spiders made webs,
exactly the way their mothers had done...
tiny, beautiful webs of gossamer lace.

And somewhere—

    in a meadow...
    in a forest...
    in a garden...

        a little spider hides,
        and waits.